A VOICE FROM THE BAOBAB TREE

Johansen N. Machume

TANZANIA EDUCATIONAL PUBLISHERS LTD

Tanzania Educational Publishers Ltd,
TEPU House,
Uganda Road,
Plot No. 45, Block MDA,
Phone: +255 685 997 583/ +255 758 147 871
Email: tepultd@yahoo.com
Website: www.tepu.co.tz
P.O. Box . 1222,
Bukoba, Tanzania.

ISBN 978 9987 671 03 8

1

Lina and her brother, Jackson, held calabashes in their hands. They went to fetch water at Kachuro stream. A strong wind blew over a bare land forming a cloudy dust.

"Oh! What a dusty day!" Lina complained.

"My eyes are aching! Jackson lamented in anger.

Both of them were tired. They had walked for two hours before reaching the stream.

"Look! A stream has dried up!" shouted Jackson in surprise.

"I can't believe it!" Lina added.

They then sat down and put aside their calabashes, completely confused.

"What shall we do? We can't live without water!" cried Jackson.

"Where else are we going to fetch some water?" Lina asked.

All of a sudden they heard a voice from a far away bush. They listened with terror. That voice was form a Baobab tree telling them:

You poor people,
You will be disturbed in your lives.
Carelessly you are clearing bushes.
Nonsensely you are creating drought.

*The Baobab tree delivering a message to
Lina and Jackson*

If we are finished,
You too will suffer.
Look, we bring rain,
We break strong wind.

Why do you cut us down?
Before being fully developed.
Mankind has to preserve us!
So that you may get our support in future.
The Baobab tree finished delivering its message.

    While still contemplating on the message passed
to them, the Baobab tree continued:

How damned you are,
Getting much profit,
At the cost of our lives.

Carelessly you burn us,
To obtain, charcoal,
You are falling us down,
To obtain plain boards.

You only care for money,
Money! Money!
You fail to understand,
The serious fate you create.

We natural trees,
We preserve sources of water.
We cure you with herbs.
We supply you with fresh air.

We natural vegetation,
Are glorious wealth.
We make strong the land.
This prevents soil erosion.

We preserve soil fertility.
Likewise water is stored.
We have many uses,
Nobody can Denny this.
So, mankind has to preserve us,
And then get our protection in return.

That message shocked them. They were sweating. They stood up and took their calabashes. Lina lead the way and her brother followed. Suddenly, they heard a terrible voice shouting to them: "Stop! I command you." It was a voice similar to that of a roaring lion.

This voice came from land on a mountain on the southern side. Jackson and Lina dropped their calabashes and trembled. They squatted and listened.

Then the land joined the tree by delivering the following message:

*The Mountain delivering a similar message to
the two children*

I join the trees,
To warn mankind,
For he has made me loose,
He has left me bare,
Due to his deeds.

Mankind has set fire on grass.
He has made me loose my fertility.
I'm of little value now,
Because rain has washed me away!

Trees are cut down for business.
Strong winds, storms and whirlwinds,
Are encouraged to blow me up!

Since God created me,
Trees have been my protector,
Grass has been my blanket,
Clouds have been my umbrella.

Distortion! What a shame!
People are starving,
Shortage of agricultural produce is alarming,
Streams are drying up,
Mankind has to protect us.

The voice from the land on the mountain stopped. Nobody said a word. Then the Baobab tree commanded the children:

Hurry up! Go home!
Tell your parents,
What you have heard.
They should understand this message:
Stop creating drought.

The land on the mountain told the Baobab tree:

Truth you are telling them,
Environment should be preserved.
Ridges should be laid across gradients,
To protect us from rain erosion.

Overstocking of their animals,
And overgrazing is ruining us.
We are completely destructed.

We are readly exposed to erosion.
To reduce soil erosion,
Mankind should destock his domestic animals.

Stop normadism.
Settle in one area,
And cultivate the land and apply appropriate
methods.
For a tree you cut, plant more than one.
Mankind has to preserve us,
So that he gets more produce for his survival.

The land concluded its message. It was past midday. Lina and Jackson held their calabashes. They ran towards their village.

Lina and Jackson reached home. They were tired and sweating. Their mother, Twelinde, was waiting for them. She was surprised to see her children return with empty calabashes. She inquired in anger, "Where is the water you went to fetch? What happened? Today I will give you no food until you bring water."

"Please mother, listen to us first, Kachuro has dried up!" Lina told her. Jackson interrupted and repeated the tree's message. He added, "The added, "The baobab tree has warned us. It has commanded us to give you this information. That people should preserve all the trees. Trees are protecting sources of water. So, they should not be cut down carelessly. When trees have been destroyed, streams will dry up and people will face hardships in looking for water."

"Even land had a message for us. It said that we should respect her since she is the mother and the true nurse of all mankind. We must stop cultivating the land carelessly. We must also reduce the number of our domestic animals. This will prevent it from turning into a desert. If this is not done, mankind will perish," Lina added.

Their mother was astonished to hear these messages. She stared at them and then asked, "Why are you misbehaving my children? Do you think I'm stupid?"

The children with the two messages returning home without water

"We are not misbehaving Mum," Jackson nodded shyly.

"Have you ever heard trees and mountains talking?" their mother asked them. They kept silent.

Lina burst out, "We are telling you the truth. For our first time we have heard a trembling voice from a Baobab tree and a Mountain. We were worried and scared. On the way back here, we also explained this incidence to the people whom we met," Jackson added, "The voices were heard by men who were cutting trees near Kachuro stream." Lina nodded in agreement with her brother.

Twelinde grunted and said, "If trees and mountains have started to talk, then goats, cows and other animals would also talk. This is strange! It must be the end of the world."

They were silent.

****

Then suddenly, two men arrived. They knocked at the door.

"Come in," Twelinde, welcomed them.

"Thank you," said Kashaija and Ganyuma.

The stepped inside the house and sat on chairs. They held matches in their hands. Both wiped sweat drops from their faces with handkerchiefs.

"How are you Twelinde?" they greeted her.

"I'm fine," she replied.

"Why are you sweating while holding matches?"

she asked them inquisitively.

"We are coming from the forest to collect poles.

Did your children tell you that we met in the forest?" asked Ganyuma.

"They didn't tell me anything," she lied.

"We have come to tell you the mysteries we have witnessed in the forest," Ganyuma explained.

"What!" Twelinde exclaimed with open eyes while pulling her chair and sat beside him.

"This morning we went to the forest near Kachuro stream. While cutting down trees for constructing my house, we heard a frightening voice from a Baobab tree. Your children were ordered to convey a message to all villagers. We were very frightened and stopped cutting down trees," explained Ganyuma.

"Then another voice from a mountain spoke to the children. We believe they have already told you that incidence," concluded Kashaija.

"They have told me the incidence but I couldn't believe them" said Twelinde slowly

"That is what has happened. We were there and heard every word," insisted Ganyuma, adding, "The Baoabab and the Mountain are grieved about mankind's misdeeds to the environment. They commanded us not to cut down trees carelessly. They also advised people to cut down the size of their domestic animals and apply appropriate cultivation methods. They added that if we do not follow their advice, streams will dry up and land will turn to desert. Consequently we will

*Ganyuma and Kashaija narrating to
Twelinde the messages*

face drought and famine," said Kashaija.

Twelinde, Ganyuma and Kashaija continued discussing the incident. Later, Ganyuma and Kashaija left Twelinde's yard. They headed to the house of village Chief.

After the two men had left, Twelinde called her children and ordered them to forget the incidences and go fetch water from Rwazi stream.

"Ooh Mum! Rwazi is very far from here," complained Lina.

"We haven't had breakfast yet! We shall go to Rwazi after lunch," Jackson requested her mother.

"We don't have water to prepare food. What will you eat?" she asked them.

"Let's go to Mum Asimwe. We will ask her to provide us with a little water," advised Lina.

"You can try, but she might be facing the same problem," her mother replied.

Jackson and her sister run to Kamanzi's residence. There, they found Dad Kamanzi sitting in a yard.

"Good afternoon Dad Kamanzi," they greeted him.

"Good afternoon, what can I help you?" he asked them.

"Where is Mum Asimwe?" Lina asked him.

"She went to Rwazi stream with her children to fetch water since morning. Since then, they haven't returned," explained Kamanzi while smoking his pipe.

Lina and Jackson were frustrated. They left dad Kamanzi's compound. Upon reaching home without water, their mother insisted that they should go to Rwazi. The children took their calabashes, disgusted and left for the stream. On their way, they met Mum Asimwe. A water pot was on her head. She was followed by her three children each one carrying a pot full of water.

"Good evening, Mum Asimwe," Jackson and Lina greeted her.

"Good evening. Where are you going?" she asked them fearfully.

"We are going to fetch water. We don't have water for drinking, cooking or washing," replied Lina.

"Go back home my beloved children. It is too late. You can't be back from Rwazi before sun set. It is dangerous.

"I shall provide you with two pots of water. Then tomorrow, in the morning, you will go to Rwazi," Asimwe told them politely. Jackson and Lina thanked her. They filled their calabashes and left for home. On arriving home, Jackson and Lina narrated to their mother the whole story. She was happy to get water and thanked Asimwe very much.

2

One evening, Mfuruki stood motionless in sorrow. He was on top of Katwetwe Mountain. Mfuruki was the Chief of Kitebwe village. No one knew his age. All his contemporaries died some decades ago. He was a gentle and most respected leader of his people.

That evening Mfuruki gazed over the lowland plains. The area was marked by grayish vegetation, being signs of drought. Coarse dusty air irritated his nostrils. He sneezed and coughed several times.

Mfuruki wondered what will happen to his people. He looked westwards. The sun was setting sluggishly beyond the horizon, reminding him past of times. He recalled the old days of Kitebwe village. He remembered the sight of green plains and lush mountains, beautiful flowers and fragrant plants all over Kachuro Valley.

Kachuro stream had been the heart of water supplies to Kitebwe people. It originated at the foot of the Mountain. The source of Kachuro was covered by a thick forest, extending downward the valley where Kachuro meandered. Kachuro was famous for its clean and cool water which trickled from under the rocks of Katwetwe Mountain. The source of Kachuro was covered by a thick forest, extending downward the valley where Kachuro meandered. Kachuro was famous for its clean and cool water which trickled from under the rocks of Katwetwe Mountain.

Mfuruki felt his legs were trembling. He sat weary on a rock. He turned to his guard Kamanzi, who stood nearby. He could not imagine what Mfuruki's thoughts were. Kamanzi had not been informed of the aim of this journey. It was in the afternoon when the Chief called him to accompany him up to the top of Katwetwe Mountain. On their way to Katwetwe, they said nothing. However, he knew Mfuruki would say something sooner or later.

"Kamanzi, our people have destroyed the beautiful environment we used to enjoy," Mfuruki started the conversation.

"You are right my Chief. Look, Kachuro has dried up. People are starving." "We don't have sufficient water," responded Kamanzi.

"Do you remember the old days? I know you were still young," said the Chief.

Silence passed between them. Then Mfuruki continued, "When I was a child, I had a friend called Byeitima.

We used to go out for hunting near Kachuro stream.

We liked rabbits. In the mornings we searched in the holes under Baobab trees and 'Bigabiro' trunks. These big trees were forbidden to be cut down, because the ancestors would curse the people. The reason for this was to preserve water and fresh air.

Chief Mfuruki showing Kamanzi destruction
of the environment

We traced holes where rabbits lived. We closed each hole with dry grass leaving one hole open. We started a fire and smoke choked the rabbit in the hole. Eventually when they came out, we caught many easily.

While Byeitima roasted the meat, I would collect mangoes, avocados and citrus fruits from nearby bushes. At the end we had a delicious feast.

In the afternoon we would return home proudly carrying the remaining catches. Today, I rarely see a boy holding a rabbit catch. Even the flora has varnished.

You hardly see butterflies of birds flying in flocks. Even bees are gone. No one will taste honey anymore! Senene used to be tasty delights but these days they are seldomly found. I suspect this is due to the scarcity of rain.

One evening we were collecting firewood in the forest. Suddenly I was bitten by a puff adder. My leg swelled as Byeitima killed the snake. He carried me home on his shoulders. My father saw us and rushed into the bushes to collect herbs. Within a short time he returned with a bunch of leaves and barks. My mother ground them and fastened it on my leg. Other herbs were hurriedly boiled. When they cooled I took several sips. I was then left to rest on the bed. In the next morning there was no pain in my leg.

If it were not for the herbs, I could have died. Today many local medicinal plants have disappeared. This is because people have been cutting down trees and burning bushes mercilessly." Mfuruki paused. He wanted Kamanzi to digest what he had told him.

"I have heard what you have said. Something has to be done to save our people," commented Kamanzi.

"Our people do not understand this problem. They have become enslaved to a new culture. I believe time will come when they will realize the mistakes they have committed," explained Chief Mfuruki thoughtfully.

"Lets go home. It is too dark to follow the way properly," Mfuruki advised.

"I'll show you the way. Just follow my footsteps," Kamanzi persuaded the Chief with a determined walk.

Kamanzi and Mfuruki went home. Kamanzi lead the way followed by Chief Mfuruki. The later decided to do something. He convened a village meeting. Thousands of people attended the meeting. Aged men and women, the blind, and the crippled also attended. Dogs barked here and there during the meeting which was held under the big eucalyptus tree.

Chief Mfuruki opened the meeting by restoring calm. Everybody listened carefully. Mfuruki stood before his people and told them, "My dear people, we are perishing. Who can survive on this drought condition? There is no sign of rain, no water and famine is looming. This introduction caused many villagers to grunt with sign of dissatisfaction. Others were surprised. When silence resumed, Chief Mfuruki continued, "I have received messages delivered to me from both the Mountain and the Baobab tree. These messages were conveyed to two children recently when were at Kachuro stream, now dry."

The majority of the people present were whispering to each other, asking themselves questions like, "Are the mountains and trees capable of speaking nowadays?" No one had the answer. A few laughed, some cursed and others intimidated that their Chief had a mental impairment.

After sometimes, they were quiet and were ready to listen to the mysteries of the Mountain and Baobab. Chief Mfuruki called in two children, who came forward before the meeting. The boy was Jackson and the girl was Lina, his sister. Mfuruki told the meeting, "If you think I'm joking, listen to these children." He then invited Jackson to speak first.

Jackson was nervous. He trembled. He had never experienced such an occasion where he was required to stand and speak in public. After a while, he cleared his

Chief Mfuruki addressing Kitebwe villagers on what to do to save the environment

throat and told the meeting, "Last week my sister Lina and I went to Kachuro to fetch water. We found it dry. It was sunny that day. Being very tired, we sat under the shade of a mango tree. Suddenly we heard a terrifying voice from a Baobab tree. The latter conveyed to us a message in a form of a command. The tree commanded us to tell you to stop clearing an burning bushes and cutting down trees carelessly around Kachuro stream and elsewhere. The Baobab said that if you disobeyed this order there would be no more water and hunger would be knocking at your doors."

All the people murmured. The Chief asked Jackson to take a seat. Mfuruki told Lina to deliver the message she heard from the Mountain. Lina said, "A voice from a Mountain claimed it was speaking on behalf of the land. We were directed to tell you that you should stop cultivating carelessly and burning bushes to avoid soil erosion. The voice continued to say that by cutting down trees this will result in less or no rain and strong winds that reduce soil fertility. We were also warned to reduce our domestic stock which loosen the soil." Then Lina stopped talking and sat down.

The meeting was silent. People realised that Chief Mfuruki had told them truth. After that Mfuruki stood before the meeting. He stared at the people with a bold face. Few people managed to hold his direct gaze. Everyone felt the mistakes that had been made against the environment. After a long silence, Chief Mfuruki continued with his speech, "My dear people, our ancestors had a saying, that, *white hairs are a sign of wisdom.* All of you here are my children and grand children. I have seen many things in my life. In my youth I enjoyed the true fortunes of our natural environment. I'm skeptical that todate none of you would have chance to enjoy similar comforts. Go and ask Kamanzi. He will tell you what I told him last week.

The younger generation should understand this. In our times we had rules and norms which preserved our environment. Things have changed. You have abandoned our traditional rules and customs. Now we are at cross roads. You don't know where to head for. Drought is alarming. Environmental destruction is accelerating.

"How are you going to resume the previous weather? Tell me now. I need you answer!" Chief Mfuruki asked the audience with a quivering voice while pointing his walking stick to them.

"Go and perform all what has been conveyed to you by the Baobab tree and the Mountain. You have become so numb that you have been commanded by land and trees," concluded Mfuruki while breathing heavily.

The meeting was closed. Everyone took his own way home.

In a few months time, Kitebwe villagers replanted natural trees. Any unsuitable vegetation was marked for cutting down and burning. The best example was the eucalyptus trees around Kachuro basin which were uprooted. Replacement was made by natural species of trees.

After several years of hardships and hard work, forests and natural vegetation resurfaced and rain started falling again. People reduced their domestic animals. Farmers applied appropriate cultivation methods. Gradually Kachuro catchments changed to green and abundant pastures were then available for livestock. Later, Kitebwe villagers also built a dam at the basin of Kachuro stream. Flora and fauna. Habitat returned. The Kachuro stream and basin, the Mountain and its neighbouring areas once again returned to its former beauty and glory.

www.ingramcontent.com/pod-product-compliance
Lightning Source LLC
Chambersburg PA
CBHW020137180726
47992CB00023B/3254